Rosetta's

Daring

Day

Rosetta's Daring Day

WRITTEN BY
LISA PAPADEMETRIOU

ILLUSTRATED BY
JUDITH HOLMES CLARKE,
ADRIENNE BROWN & CHARLES PICKENS

A STEPPING STONE BOOK™
RANDOM HOUSE 🏠 NEW YORK

Library of Congress Cataloging-in-Publication Data

Papademetriou, Lisa.

Rosetta's daring day / written by Lisa Papademetriou ; illustrated by
Judith Holmes Clarke, Adrienne Brown & Charles Pickens.

p. cm.

"A Stepping Stone book."

Summary: Rosetta, a dainty garden-talent fairy, and her friend Fawn, a
rough-and-tumble animal-talent fairy, face their fears when Fawn agrees
to dress up for a fancy dinner with the queen and Rosetta spends the
next day doing Fawn's favorite things.

ISBN 978-0-7364-2509-4 (pbk.)

[*1. Fairies—Fiction. 2. Individuality—Fiction. 3. Fear—Fiction.*]
*I. Clarke, Judith, ill. II. Brown, Adrienne, ill. III. Pickens, Charles, ill.
IV. Title.*

PZ7.P1954Ros 2009

[Fic]—dc22   2007035978

www.randomhouse.com/kids/disney

Printed in the United States of America

10 9 8 7 6 5 4 3 2 1

All About Fairies

IF YOU HEAD toward the second star on your right and fly straight on till morning, you'll come to Never Land, a magical island where mermaids play and children never grow up.

When you arrive, you might hear something like the tinkling of little bells. Follow that sound and you'll find Pixie Hollow, the secret heart of Never Land.

A great old maple tree grows in Pixie Hollow, and in it live hundreds of fairies and sparrow men. Some of them can do water magic, others can fly like the wind, and still others can speak to animals. You see, Pixie Hollow is the Never fairies' kingdom, and each fairy who lives there has a special, extraordinary talent.

Not far from the Home Tree, nestled in the branches of a hawthorn, is Mother Dove, the most magical creature of all. She sits on her egg, watching over the fairies, who in turn watch over her. For as long as Mother Dove's egg stays well and whole, no one in Never Land will ever grow old.

Once, Mother Dove's egg *was* broken. But we are not telling the story of the egg here. Now it is time for Rosetta's tale. . . .

Rosetta's

Daring

Day

1

"ROSETTA! COME QUICK!" Fawn fluttered wildly into the garden. "Rosetta! Rose—"

Rosetta's head was deep inside a lily's bloom when she heard Fawn calling her. Rosetta was a garden-talent fairy and had been stirring up the pollen. She popped her head out. "What is it?"

When Fawn caught sight of her friend, she tried to stop. But she was going too fast. She crashed into a bright red rose. Brilliant scarlet petals exploded everywhere.

"My rose!" Rosetta cried. She flew past Fawn and over to the flower. Half its petals were gone. Rosetta planted a hand on her hip. "Fawn, what are you doing?" she demanded.

"Oops!" Fawn started picking up the red petals. "It's just that we're about to start a game of acorn ball."

"So?" Rosetta tossed her long, red hair.

"So maybe you want to join us?" Fawn asked. She handed the flower petals to Rosetta. "Everyone's going to be there. Tink and Fira and Rani and—"

"Not really, Fawn," Rosetta said. Rosetta didn't care for games or sports.

She liked beautiful things, such as flowers and frilly dresses and delicate petal shoes. "I've got a lot of work to do in the garden."

"What work?" Fawn gave Rosetta a doubtful look. In Rosetta's flower patch, everything was in perfect order. The blue irises grew in straight rows. The pink and white lilies stood tall on their green stalks. The roses were in full bloom . . . well, all except for the one Fawn had run into. "Everything looks perfect," Fawn said.

Rosetta sighed. "You're *such* an animal talent," she said. "Anyone can see that the garden is a *disaster!*"

Rosetta didn't really think that her garden was a mess. In fact, she thought it looked quite pretty. She was particularly proud of the deep blue morning glories. But Rosetta didn't want to play acorn ball. It meant flying here and there and tossing an acorn around and trying to tag other fairies. The last time she had played, her hair had gotten terribly tangled.

"A disaster?" Fawn blinked in surprise. "It looks beautiful to me."

Rosetta couldn't help a small proud smile. "You think so?" Her glow turned as pink as her rose-petal dress. She cleared her throat. "Well, never mind. I've still got a lot of work to do."

"Are you sure you're not scared to play acorn ball?" Fawn asked. She tapped her foot in midair.

"I don't know what you're talking about!" Rosetta huffed.

"Maybe I'm talking about the time you missed the easy catch—and our team beat yours thirty-one to three." Fawn lifted her eyebrows.

Rosetta's glow reddened at the memory. She couldn't believe she'd missed the ball! It had rolled right through her hands—and broken three of her fingernails! After that, she had sworn she'd never play again. "It's not that at all," Rosetta fibbed. "I just have a lot to do."

"Maybe I could help you," Fawn suggested. "If we worked together, we would get done faster. Then you could play with us."

Rosetta flew to the end of the row of daffodils, where a careless bunny had trampled a leaf. "If you really want to help me, tell the rabbits to stay out of my garden!" She propped the leaf up with a twig and sprinkled it with water.

Fawn smiled. "I can tell them, but I doubt they'll listen," she said. "Rabbits have big ears, but they also have minds of their own. They don't like getting bossed around. So, Rosetta, how about it—do you want me to help you pull some weeds?"

Rosetta harrumphed. "You don't know the difference between a weed and a prize orchid!"

"That's true," Fawn said with a sigh. She was clearly disappointed. Rosetta felt a stab of guilt for hurting her friend's feelings.

"It's okay, Fawn," Rosetta said. "Working in the garden is my talent, just like working with animals is yours. Go ahead and play acorn ball. Then you can come back and tell me all about it. It will be like I was there." *Without the messy hair*, she added silently.

Fawn grinned. "All right, I will!" She turned a flip in the air, then zipped off toward the field near the Home Tree. "I'll be back soon!" she called over her shoulder.

Rosetta waved one of the rose petals like a leafkerchief at her friend. Then she flew to the morning glories to check the shady side of the garden.

In the shadow of a nearby maple tree was a green patch that Rosetta loved. It was always cool, even when the sun was hot. A special, silvery fern grew there. It had just poked up from the earth and was curled into tight fists. They were called fiddleheads at this stage. They could be cooked up in the kitchen into a crisp, delicious treat.

But Rosetta wouldn't let anyone pick the fiddleheads. She loved these ferns. Not only did the leaves look like hearts, but the plants gave off a clean, fresh scent that was as lovely as any flower's.

Rosetta perched atop a rock among the morning glories. "Ahh," she said. "The garden is so quiet. So peaceful. So—"

A loud noise cut through the silent garden. It was a squirrel making quite a racket.

"Oh, be quiet!" Rosetta said to the squirrel. She could see him standing on a tree limb overhead. He swished his fluffy red tail.

"Can't you see that I'm trying to

have a relaxing moment in my garden?" Rosetta shouted.

But the squirrel didn't give up. He ran along the limb, back and forth, chattering nonstop. Rosetta plugged her ears. It didn't help. She could hear the squirrel right through her fingers.

"You can quit trying to talk to me. I'm not an animal talent." Rosetta folded her arms across her chest. "I can't understand a word you're saying, and I wouldn't care even if I could."

She waved her arms in an attempt to scare the squirrel away. It didn't have any effect. In fact, the squirrel seemed to be making more noise now than before.

Rosetta let out a frustrated sigh. "That's it. This crazy squirrel is driving

me nuts!" There was only one solution. She'd have to go find Fawn. Maybe an animal talent could make this animal go chatter in another maple tree.

2

"I GOT IT!" Fawn shouted. She flew up to meet the acorn that arced through the air. "I got it!"

"Hurry, Tink!" Rani cried. Tinker Bell raced to tag a knot in a tall oak tree. Once she'd touched the knot, she zipped toward the branch above it. If she could circle the branch twice before Fawn caught the acorn, her team would get a point. If Fawn missed the acorn, Tink's team would get three points.

"I got it!" Fawn shouted again.

"You can do it, Fawn!" Rani yelled.

"Rani, who are you rooting for?" Fira called down to her friend.

Rani shrugged and leaned back against a root. "Everyone!" she said.

Rani was the only fairy in Pixie Hollow who didn't have wings. Brother Dove flew her wherever she needed to go, or else she walked. She never played acorn ball. It was too difficult without her own wings. But she loved to watch.

Above, the acorn flew just beyond Fawn's grasp. Grunting, she flapped her wings with a final effort—

"Look out!" Rani cried. But nothing

could stop Fawn . . . or Rosetta. They crashed right into each other.

Shooting past Fawn's hand, the acorn dropped to the ground. Tinker Bell rounded the branch for the second time. The fairies on Tink's team cheered.

"Rosetta?" Fawn rubbed her side. Rosetta had nearly knocked her over!

"What are you doing? Did you come to join our game?"

"No, no!" Rosetta shook her head. It was throbbing where Fawn's elbow had knocked it. She didn't understand how Fawn could play acorn ball. It was downright dangerous! But there was no time to argue about it. "I need your help. There's a squirrel who is driving me crazy! Can you come get rid of him?"

"What?" Fawn asked. "You interrupted our game to ask me to get rid of a squirrel?"

"I thought you said you wanted to help me!" Rosetta wailed. "This squirrel is acting really weird." *And he's really annoying*, she added silently.

"Hmm." Fawn thought for a moment.

"Maybe something is wrong. Okay, Rosetta, I'll go and talk to the squirrel." She flew off toward Rosetta's garden.

"Hey, Fawn! Where are you going?" Tinker Bell called.

"Rosetta's got a squirrel problem!" Fawn shouted over her shoulder. "I'll be back soon!"

"A squirrel problem?" Rani repeated. "I'll come with you." Getting to her feet, she whistled for Brother Dove. In a heartbeat, the bird appeared. Rani climbed onto his back. They followed Fawn and Rosetta to see what was the matter with the squirrel.

"There he is!" Rosetta pointed at the squirrel. At the sight of the fairies, he had run out to the edge of a branch and started chattering madly at them. "See? He's crazy."

"He looks upset, not crazy," Fawn remarked. The fairies flew closer to the animal.

The squirrel chattered again as his tail twitched from side to side.

"What?" Fawn cried. "A fire?" She chattered back in Squirrel.

Rosetta's heart froze. A fire? In the forest? It could burn down all of Pixie Hollow!

Fawn said something else. The squirrel clambered down the maple trunk and bounded through the forest. Fawn zipped after him.

"What's going on?" Rosetta asked. She flew close behind Fawn. Rani and

Brother Dove were right on her heels.

"There's a fire!" Fawn said. "Rani, we'll need your help." Rani was a water-talent fairy. If anyone could help with a fire, it was she.

"Hurry, Brother Dove!" Rani whispered. The bird flew like an arrow.

Soon the fairies smelled smoke. Then they saw the fire. It had started in a small bush. A nearby tree was burned black at the trunk. When Rosetta saw it, she knew what had happened. The tree had been struck by lightning. The sparks must have smoldered for a while until the bush caught fire.

Orange flames licked at the bush. Rani didn't waste any time. She darted to a nearby puddle and threw fairy dust onto it. Instantly, a jet of water sprang up. Rani directed it toward the flames.

Rosetta coughed and waved her hand in front of her face. She hated the smell of smoke. If it got into her hair, she'd smell horrible for days. She flew a short distance away from the fire.

Water hissed as Rani's jet touched the flames, but it wasn't enough to stop the fire. "It's sending up sparks!" Rani cried. "The fire could spread!"

"Rosetta, gather some dew moss!" Fawn shouted. "You can throw it on the fire! I'll be back!"

"Where are you going?" Rosetta called, but it was too late. Her friend was already gone.

Rosetta hesitated. She really didn't

want to gather dew moss. It was dirty, for one thing. Plus it would stain her hands green.

Maybe if I wait just another moment, Rani will put out the fire, Rosetta thought. *Then they won't need me to gather moss.*

Brother Dove swooped toward the flames, and Rani sent up another glittering jet of water. The fire was still burning.

It really looks like she needs my help, Rosetta thought. She was just about to fly off to find some moss when she heard a whoop.

"Ya-hoo!" Fawn hooted. The animal-talent fairy bounded toward the fire on the back of a brown rabbit. Eight more rabbits hopped behind them. The rabbits

leaped into the smoke and used their enormous feet to crush the orange embers that had flown up from the bush.

Rani raised her arms again. One, two, three, four, *five* jets of water blasted the flames. With a final hiss, the last flicker died out. A cottontail stamped on it, just to be sure.

"We did it!" Fawn wrapped her arms around the rabbit's neck and buried her face in its fur. The rabbit's ear twitched. Fawn let the bunny go and flew toward Rani. She was looking at Brother Dove's wing.

"Is he okay?" Fawn asked.

"His feathers are a little scorched, but he's all right," Rani said. "We're fine."

"So is Pixie Hollow, thanks to you!" Fawn pulled Rani into a tight hug. "And to this squirrel!" She patted the animal on the shoulder and said something to him in Squirrel.

The rabbits began to hop away.

Fawn called something to them in Rabbit.

"Oh, Fawn, can you tell them not to trample my flowers?" Rosetta asked. "Since they're all here?"

Fawn and Rani turned to face Rosetta. Neither one of them was smiling. "What happened to the dew moss?" Fawn asked.

Rosetta blushed rose pink. "Well, I—I couldn't find any." *Because I didn't look*, she added to herself.

"Hmm," Fawn said.

"Hmm," Rani said, too.

"Besides, it looked like you had the fire under control," Rosetta said.

"Well, the rabbits are gone," Fawn pointed out. "Maybe I'll mention it to them later."

Fawn didn't sound like she really wanted to mention it. Rosetta sighed. *That is so like Fawn. She doesn't even care about my flowers. Some fairies are just so selfish!*

3

ROSETTA YAWNED AND opened one eye. Light streamed in through the Queen Anne's lace curtains over her bedroom window. She folded down her rabbit-fur blanket. The blanket had been made by the weaving-talent fairies. After the animal talents brushed the rabbits, the weaving talents collected the fur. Rosetta's blanket was as soft and warm as a baby bunny. She hated getting out of bed—even though she didn't like rabbits much.

At the window, a black and white butterfly caught Rosetta's eye. Its wings opened and closed slowly, as if it was waiting for her to notice it. Rosetta looked more closely. The butterfly was made out of birch bark!

"Oh, my goodness!" Rosetta cried. She hurried to the window. "It's a message from Queen Clarion!"

Even though no one else was in the room, Rosetta smoothed her hair and tidied her nightgown before holding up her hand. The birch bark–paper butterfly landed lightly on her fingers and unfolded itself into a formal invitation. Rosetta read it eagerly.

Calling all fairies and sparrow men:
Queen Clarion requests your presence
at a dinner to honor those who saved
Pixie Hollow from a forest fire.

We will meet in Buttercup Canyon.

"Dinner with the queen!" Rosetta cried. She dropped the invitation onto her bed. "And it's tonight! What in Never Land will I wear?"

Thumpthumpthump! Someone was pounding on Rosetta's door. "It's me!" Fawn shouted. "I need to talk to you!" Fawn flung open the door and flew inside.

"Careful!" Rosetta cried as one of

the tiny glass perfume bottles on her bureau fell over.

"Oops!" Fawn managed to catch the bottle just before it landed on the floor.

Lucky she's such a fast flier, Rosetta thought. *Especially for someone who isn't a fast-flying talent.*

Fawn put the perfume back in its place and came over to her friend. She waved the invitation under Rosetta's nose. "Did you see this?" she demanded.

"Yes! Isn't it wonderful?" Rosetta's face broke into a huge smile.

"Wonderful?" Fawn shrieked. "How can you say it's wonderful? We're going to have to get dressed up!"

"Well, of course." Rosetta darted to her mirror to check her reflection.

"But I don't want to get dressed up," Fawn complained. "I don't want to go to a special dinner!"

"Don't be ridiculous," Rosetta said. She pulled a porcupine-quill comb through her tangled hair. "It's dinner with the queen!" Honestly, sometimes Rosetta didn't understand her tomboyish friend at all.

"Exactly!" Fawn griped. She picked up one of the small feathers from Rosetta's collection. Then she put it back down askew. "Dinner with lots of extra forks. Who wants that? I'd rather brush the skunks!"

Rosetta smoothed the delicate blue feather back into place. "You don't mean that."

"Sure I do!" Fawn fluttered toward the ceiling. "Why does the queen have to throw a fancy dinner? Why can't we just play a fun game of pea shoot?"

"Because pea shoot isn't fun," Rosetta retorted.

"It's a lot more fun than getting dressed up," Fawn said.

"How would you even know whether getting dressed up is fun?" Rosetta asked. "You've never done it!"

Fawn folded her arms across her chest. "Well, how would you know that pea shoot isn't fun?" she replied. "I've never seen *you* try it."

"Well, I—well—" Rosetta sputtered, then stopped herself. Fawn had a point. She had never played pea shoot.

But she had watched the fairies lobbing peas at each other. It didn't look like something she would enjoy.

The two fairies stared at each other for a moment.

"All right, Fawn," Rosetta said at last. "I'll make a deal with you. First you come to Queen Clarion's special dinner tonight."

Fawn groaned and landed on Rosetta's bed with a plop. She put her hands to her head.

"I'll help you pick out something to wear," Rosetta promised.

"What kind of a deal is that?" Fawn demanded.

"I'm not finished. Then tomorrow, I'll do anything you'd like to do," said

Rosetta. "Play pea shoot or acorn ball, or whatever."

Fawn let out a whoop. "Then you'll see that pea shoot is way more fun than going to a fancy dinner!" She flipped in midair.

"No," Rosetta said, correcting her. "*You'll* see how much fun it is to put on a beautiful outfit and look pretty. Now, get dressed. We can go to the sewing talents and choose something to wear."

Fawn looked down at her plain leggings. "I *am* dressed," she said.

"Oh," Rosetta said. She'd thought that Fawn was still wearing her pajamas. She cleared her throat. "Well, then— give me a minute to get dressed."

Fawn sighed. "You've never been able

to get dressed in a minute in your life."

"Good point," Rosetta agreed. She started to comb her hair again. "Come back in an hour."

Fawn looked doubtful.

"Okay, an hour and a half," Rosetta said. "But don't be late! We'll need as much time as possible to get ready!"

4

"I LOVE IT!" Rosetta cried.

She turned in front of the full-length mirror, admiring herself. The sewing-talent fairies had just pulled a dress made of violets over her head. The violets were set in frills that went from deep purple at the bottom to pale purple at the top. Feathery, purple-fringed irises puffed out at the sleeves. "The purple really brings out the color of my eyes, don't you think?"

"It definitely does," Thimble agreed.

"I think the hemline could be a bit higher," Hawthorn suggested.

"Oh, nonsense," Rosetta told her. "It's a perfect fit! Fawn!" she called. "Are you having any luck with that dress?"

Fawn pulled aside the green and white leaf that served as a dressing room curtain and flew into the center of the room. She was wearing a lacy white dress made of dandelion fluff.

"You look gorgeous!" Rosetta cried. She circled her friend to see her from all sides. "Doesn't she look gorgeous?"

"Yes, oh, yes." The sewing-talent fairies agreed that Fawn looked beautiful.

Fawn scratched at her waist. "It's itchy," she complained.

"Oh, Fawn!" Rosetta shook her head. "First the rose-petal dress was too poufy. Then the blue snapdragon gown pinched under the arm. Then the poppy dress was too long and got caught in your wings!" She gave an exasperated sigh.

Fawn shrugged. "I just want to be comfortable."

"Fancy dresses aren't comfortable," Rosetta shot back. "They're beautiful. And look at yourself." Taking her friend by the hand, Rosetta led her to the mirror. "You have to admit that you look amazing."

Fawn blinked in surprise at her reflection. The dress was as white as a fluffy cloud, and it sparkled with tiny dewdrops that looked like diamonds. Weaving-talent fairies had made a sash of pale pink silk strands from a red Never spider. The sash tied in the back with a huge pink bow. It almost looked like a second, smaller set of fairy wings. The gown was absolutely breathtaking.

"It *is* very pretty," Fawn admitted.

"That's it." Rosetta nodded in approval. "That's the dress. So stop scratching."

"But it itches!" Fawn said again.

"Don't think about it," Rosetta commanded. "Just think about how pretty you look. That makes the itching go away."

Fawn scrunched up her face, trying

hard to concentrate on how pretty she looked. "I still itch."

"You'll get used to it." Rosetta shrugged. "Are you ready to go to the shoemaking talent?"

"Rosetta, my wings are tired!" Fawn moaned. "We've already picked out jewelry, perfume, and stockings!"

"And we still have to go to the hair-dressing talent, too! Oh, come on." Rosetta waved her hand as though she were shooing away a fly. "I don't understand you, Fawn. You can spend all day trooping through the forest and not get tired!"

"But that's different."

"It sure is," Rosetta agreed. "You don't get muddy and dirty trying on perfume!" She turned to the sewing-talent fairies. "We'll take these dresses."

"We'll see you at dinner!" Thimble called as Rosetta and Fawn flew out the door.

An hour later, Rosetta was satisfied. They had everything they needed for the dinner. "I can't believe I got a pair of pink shoes," Fawn said. She was carrying three huge leaf bags and a shoe box.

"They were the most beautiful shoes there," Rosetta insisted. "I was sure you would like them. Nothing is more comfortable than rose-petal slippers."

"Well, they are comfortable," Fawn admitted. The pale pink shoes were nestled in a puff of mouse fur inside the box under her right arm. "But I could never run in them."

"You're not going to be running at the queen's dinner," Rosetta pointed out. "At least, I hope not," she added under her breath.

"What if some of the fairies want to play a game of no-wings tag?" Fawn asked.

Rosetta groaned. "Then you'll play it tomorrow—when *you* choose what we do," she said.

Fawn sighed. Just then, a large golden dragonfly darted past them. It was flying so fast that Rosetta felt the breeze from its wings against her face.

"Oh, no, you don't, Flitterwing!"

Fawn called after the dragonfly. "You can't beat me this time!" With a whoop, she dropped her bags and her box and took off after the golden insect.

"Fawn!" Rosetta screeched. But Fawn wasn't listening.

Then Rosetta noticed the leaf bags fluttering toward the ground. They were headed right for a puddle. "Not the shoes!" she cried.

With a burst of speed she hadn't known she was capable of, she swooped in to catch the rose-petal slippers. "Gotcha!" Rosetta collected the bags as they floated past her.

Fawn and the dragonfly wound around a white birch tree in a spiral.

"You might have won the last race,"

Fawn shouted, "but I'll win this one!"

The dragonfly buzzed and pulled ahead. It zoomed over the top branch and dove toward a clump of blue pansies. Fawn stayed with it. She was so close, she could almost touch its wings!

Rosetta watched Fawn race the dragonfly. "Oooh," she said. She was furious at Fawn for her behavior. "That fairy is going to get all dirty!" And there wasn't time for Fawn to take another bath. "I'd better stop her before she makes a mess of herself," Rosetta said. She zipped toward the blue pansies.

"Fawn!" Rosetta yelled. She dropped between her friend and the pansies and held out both hands.

Fawn stopped short.

Rosetta was loaded down with bags and Fawn's box. Her face was stormy.

Fawn cleared her throat. "Rosetta!" she squeaked. "See you some other time, Flitterwing," Fawn told the dragonfly. It buzzed away.

Rosetta thrust the bags at her friend. "You dropped these," she said.

"Oops." Sheepishly, Fawn took the bags.

Rosetta's anger faded. She knew that her friend couldn't help getting excited when a dragonfly wanted to race. All the animal-talent fairies were like that—and none more than Fawn. But still—it was too silly. "You can't just go dragonfly racing when we have things to do," Rosetta scolded.

"You're right," Fawn admitted. "I didn't mean to."

"It's okay," Rosetta told her. "But let's hurry. We still have to get our hair done and get dressed before dinner." She started off toward the Home Tree. Would Fawn ever get the hang of having Rosetta's kind of fun?

PINK AND GOLD clouds hovered over Buttercup Canyon. Thousands of tiny pink and yellow flowers carpeted the valley. They seemed to shine in the fading light.

At the edge of the canyon, dozens upon dozens of fireflies glowed over crisp white tablecloths set with plates of gleaming mother-of-pearl. The tables were beginning to fill up with fairies.

Rosetta's eyes were wide as she glanced around. "Oh, look," she said with a gasp. "There's Fira! Her cardinal-feather dress is gorgeous! Rani and Tink are with her. I just love what Tink's done with her hair!"

Fawn trailed behind her friend. "I'm itchy," she said.

"Oh, stop complaining," Rosetta told her. Waving her hands, she called, "Fira! Tink! Rani! Over here!"

"Brass buckles, Fawn!" Tink cried. She flew right past Rosetta. "You look so beautiful! I almost didn't know it was you."

"Is that dress made of dandelion fluff?" Fira gushed.

Rani gave Fawn an enormous smile. "It looks great on you."

Fawn's glow—already ruddy in the light from the setting sun—turned even pinker. "Rosetta helped me pick it out," she said.

Rosetta beamed.

"Wow, Rosetta," Tink said, "Fawn looks great!"

Clearing her throat, Rosetta struck a pose. *And now,* she thought, *it's time for someone to notice* my *dress!*

Vidia flew over to join the crowd. "Well, well, what have we here?" she asked. "Rosetta, darling, what in Never Land are you wearing? You look like a plum."

Rosetta glared at Vidia. Vidia was

the meanest fairy in Pixie Hollow.

"Of course, I only mean that plums are sweet, dearest," Vidia said with a smirk. "And look at Fawn. I'm shocked. You look simply magical, Fawn, you really do."

Rosetta waited for Vidia to add an insult. But the insult never came.

"I do?" Fawn asked finally.

"She does?" Rani repeated.

"Vidia, I don't think I've ever heard you give anyone a compliment before," Fira said.

Vidia's smile slithered up one side of her face. "There's a first time for everything, darling." And with that, she flew off to sit at a table by herself.

Rosetta frowned. This party was not

going the way she had planned. No one had noticed her lovely dress. Or her darling little slippers.

And that Vidia had complimented Fawn only made Rosetta feel worse.

Just then, Grace, one of the queen's helpers, flew over. In a formal voice, she said, "Queen Clarion would like to invite you to sit at her table."

Rosetta's heart pattered double-time. Sit with the queen! What an honor!

"That's nice, but we're already sitting with our friends," Fawn said.

Rosetta gaped in surprise. "Wait!" she cried, but it was too late. Grace had flown away.

Rosetta turned to Fawn. "Why did you do that?" she demanded.

"Don't you want to sit with Tink, Rani, and Fira?" Fawn asked.

"You just insulted the queen!" Rosetta cried.

"She doesn't look insulted," Tink said.

Rosetta saw that Queen Clarion herself was flying over. A delicate crown sparkled in the queen's golden hair, and she wore a lovely yellow ruffled daffodil dress. Whenever Rosetta saw the queen, she became terribly nervous. Rosetta felt that Queen Clarion was the most beautiful fairy who had ever lived.

"Fawn, I understand that you want to eat dinner with your friends," the queen said in her gentle voice. "I hope you don't mind if I join you."

"We'd be honored!" Rosetta cried. She pulled out the chair beside hers.

Queen Clarion settled between Rosetta and Fawn. Rani sat at the end of the table with Brother Dove nestled beside her.

I'm sitting next to Queen Clarion! Rosetta thought giddily. She searched her mind for something clever to say. She wanted to impress the queen with her wittiness. But she couldn't think of a single thing.

"Fawn, your dress is lovely," Queen Clarion said.

Rosetta glowed with pride.

"It's very itchy," Fawn said.

Rosetta slapped her own forehead. She'd told Fawn a hundred times not to say anything embarrassing in front of the queen!

Queen Clarion just laughed her sparkly laugh. "My shoes are too tight," she admitted.

A serving talent flew over. She was carrying an enormous soup tureen. With a smile, she ladled some squash-blossom soup into Fawn's bowl.

Please don't slurp, Rosetta begged silently. She and Fawn hadn't had time to practice sipping soup.

But Fawn *did* slurp. A drip of soup ran down her chin. She used the back of her hand to wipe it off.

Rosetta bit her lip and forced herself not to say anything. She hoped the queen noticed that *she* wasn't slurping.

"It looks like the queen and Fawn are having a nice chat," Fira whispered to Rosetta.

Rosetta had to admit that it was true. The queen had laughed heartily at one of Fawn's stories about a game of butterfly tag. She had even chimed in with a story of her own about a time she had tried to ride a moth.

After a while, the queen stood up. "Attention, everyone," she called, tapping her glass.

A hush fell over the fairies. They turned to look at their queen.

"We're gathered here tonight to honor certain fairies," Queen Clarion announced. "As you all know, there was a fire at the edge of the forest." A murmur rippled through the crowd. "It could have burned all of Pixie Hollow, if it weren't for some very brave fairies."

Rosetta sat up a little in her chair.

"First there was the fairy who used her water talent to fight the flames," the queen said. "Step forward, Rani."

The queen hung a silver necklace around Rani's neck. Rani smiled. Her blue eyes brimmed with happy tears.

"Rani could not have put out the fire without help," the queen went on. "Brother Dove flew close to the flames to make sure the job got done."

Queen Clarion hung a silver necklace around his neck.

"And we are grateful to Fawn," the queen said. "She realized that there was a fire and brought a herd of rabbits to stamp out the sparks."

Fawn bowed her head so that the queen could slide a silver necklace over it. The fairies roared their approval. The cheers echoed through Buttercup Canyon.

Rosetta clapped with the others. Then she turned to Queen Clarion, her face tilted up, her eyes dancing. She knew what was coming next.

"I'm glad you all could come to this very special dinner," Queen Clarion said. "It's truly wonderful to honor these fairies for their good deeds."

Rosetta sat at the table, stunned. She was still waiting for the queen to mention her name. After all, she was the one who'd flown to get Fawn. And she would have helped put out the fire . . . if she could have done something besides collect dew moss. Surely, she should get some credit for trying—shouldn't she?

But the queen had already flown off. The ceremony was over. Fairies were leaving for the Home Tree.

"Isn't it pretty?" Fawn asked. She

held the silver necklace up to the moonlight.

"Beautiful!" Fira said.

"I can't believe she gave one to each of us!" Rani said.

"Rosetta, you were right!" Fawn cried. "This really was a fun night!"

Rosetta sighed. Fun? She hadn't thought it was very fun at all. Nobody had noticed her dress—except Vidia, who had said something nasty. The queen had barely spoken to her. And she was the only one who had been at the fire who hadn't gotten a silver necklace!

She wanted to be happy for Fawn. She wanted to be, but she wasn't.

6

"WAKE UP, SLEEPYHEAD!" Fawn sang as she flew into Rosetta's room. "It's time to have some fun!"

Groaning, Rosetta buried her head under her fluffy pillow. Leave it to Fawn to wake her up early for their day together. Already it was off to a bad start.

Fawn reached down and yanked the pillow off Rosetta's head. "Don't tell me that you're going to back out on your promise, Rosetta."

Rosetta squinted up at her friend. "I never go back on my promises," she said.

"Good," Fawn replied.

"But don't you think we should wait until tomorrow?" Rosetta suggested. She didn't want to get out from under her comfortable blankets just to play acorn ball or race dragonflies, or whatever it was that Fawn had in mind. "I'm a little tired from the party last night—"

Fawn laughed. "You won't feel tired once you see what I've got planned!"

With a doubtful look, Rosetta asked, "What is it?"

"You'll see!" Fawn said, her eyes twinkling.

Rosetta cleared her throat. "We're not going to do anything"—she searched for the right word—"gross . . . are we?"

Fawn laughed. "Of course not! Now, hurry and get dressed. We don't want to waste the whole day!"

Rosetta sighed. It was clear that Fawn wasn't going to give her any hints about her plans for the day. Rosetta pulled on a fresh rose-petal skirt and blouse but stopped before putting on her shoes.

Should she wear her new pair—the violet petals lined with white rabbit fur? They were very beautiful but also very comfortable. *Well, Fawn said we won't be doing anything gross*, Rosetta thought. She slipped her toes into the shoes.

Then she brushed her hair, straightened her wings, and tidied her bed. "All right," she said at last, "I'm ready now. Where are we off to?"

"Not so fast," Fawn said. "First you have to put on this blindfold." She held out a scarf made from a tender blade of grass.

Rosetta frowned at the scarf. "How can I fly wearing a blindfold?" she asked. "I'll run into a tree!"

"Don't worry. I'll lead you." Fawn tied the scarf over Rosetta's eyes. "Can you see?" she asked.

"Nothing but darkness," Rosetta replied.

"Perfect!" Fawn giggled. Tugging on Rosetta's hand, she pulled her through the Home Tree and out into the center of Pixie Hollow. Fawn was very careful to watch out for Rosetta. "A little to the left," she said as Rosetta neared a tall sunflower. "Now dip downward a bit," she said when they flew under a branch.

At first, Rosetta didn't like being blindfolded at all. But Fawn led her safely around obstacles, and she began to relax. Soon she found that she could use her other senses to guess where they were going.

She felt the sun on her face. That meant they were headed east. Then she smelled the sweet scent of freshly baked poppy puff rolls. *Maybe we're going to gather poppies for the bakers!* she thought.

"Are we going to the kitchen?" Rosetta asked hopefully.

"Flying past it," Fawn said.

Rosetta's nose began to twitch again. "I smell roses!" she cried happily. Roses were, of course, her favorite flowers. "Are we going to my garden for a game of butterfly tag?"

"We won't be too far away from

your garden," Fawn answered playfully, pulling Rosetta along, "but that's not where we're going."

After a while, Rosetta heard the bubbling of rushing water. That could only mean one thing. "Are we going to spend the day at Havendish Stream?"

"You've guessed it!" Fawn cried. She led Rosetta to a seat on the bank.

"Oh, what fun!" Rosetta clapped her hands. She pictured herself floating along on a leaf boat, enjoying the sun as Fawn pointed out the pretty fish that swam below. Of course! That was something they would both enjoy. "Fawn, you're brilliant! You're absolutely—"

Rosetta's words stuck in her throat when Fawn pulled away her blindfold.

Sitting in the water at the bank of the stream were two enormous green bullfrogs. Both were wearing harnesses made of bark rope.

"*Ribbit!*" one of them said.

"We're going frog-riding!" Fawn said with a whoop.

Frog-riding? "I thought you said we weren't going to do anything gross!" Rosetta wailed.

"What's gross about frogs?" Fawn asked. "They spend most of their time in the water. They're very clean!"

One of the frogs seemed to agree. "*Ribbit!*"

Rosetta stared at her friend. Fawn was completely serious. She believed that frog-riding was a fun, nongross activity. Fawn's eyes were shining, and her cheeks were pink with excitement. *I can't refuse to go*, Rosetta thought. *I promised I'd do whatever she wanted.*

Me and my big mouth.

Fawn splashed through the ankle-deep
water toward the bullfrogs. Rosetta
waited on the bank. "I've never been
frog-riding," she said.

"It's easy!" Fawn held out the reins
attached to the harness on the smaller
frog. "I'll show you."

Rosetta didn't want to ruin her new
shoes, so she fluttered toward the frog.

"Just drop into the saddle." Fawn gestured toward the almond shell on the frog's back.

Rosetta hovered for a moment, unsure. "Where do I put my feet?"

"On the frog," Fawn said. "Like this!" With a quick move, she grabbed the reins and hauled herself into the saddle. Her feet rested lightly on the frog's shoulders.

Rosetta grimaced. The frogs were bright green and had a slight sheen. *I don't want my new shoes to touch that slimy frog,* she thought. But she didn't want to say that to Fawn. "All right," she said at last. She dropped daintily into the almond shell.

"See?" Fawn grinned at her friend.

"Nothing to be afraid of. It's easy!"

The frog shifted beneath Rosetta. "Eek!" she cried. She windmilled her arms, then leaned forward and grabbed the frog's neck.

"*Ribbit!*" said the frog.

The frog's skin was cool and damp. Looking down, Rosetta found herself staring into a giant yellow eye. "Yikes!" she shouted.

"You're scaring Strongjump," Fawn said. She croaked at him in Frog. "I just told him to calm down," she explained. "You're not going to hurt him."

"He's afraid of *me?*" Rosetta asked. She straightened up in the saddle. *What's Strongjump worried about?* she wondered. After all, he wasn't wearing pretty new shoes that might get ruined on a crazy frog ride!

"If you want Strongjump to go right, pull the reins to the right," Fawn explained. "If you want to go left, pull the reins left."

"And what if I want to stop and get off?" Rosetta muttered.

"Then pull the reins toward you," Fawn told her. "And if you want him to go faster, just give him a little poke—like this!" She reached out and touched Strongjump's side.

"*Ribbit!*" Strongjump took a giant leap forward.

He landed with a plop and a splash on a nearby lily pad. Rosetta grabbed the reins more tightly.

"Come on, Swiftlegs!" Fawn called to her frog. "Let's go!"

Swiftlegs hopped along the edge of Havendish Stream. He sent up a spray of water around him. The drops sparkled in the sunlight.

Strongjump leaped after Swiftlegs. Rosetta felt as if she were trying to fly in a windstorm. "Yikes!" she cried.

"Just hang on!" Fawn shouted. Swiftlegs led the way from stone to stone, then across the stream on lily pads. "Plant your feet. That will keep you steady!"

Rosetta jammed her feet against Strongjump's sides and clung to the reins for dear life. She squeezed her eyes shut. "Tell me when it's over!"

Fawn laughed. "You're a natural frog-rider!"

"I am?" Rosetta opened one eye wide enough to see a gold and black bumblebee buzz into a bright purple water lily. Silver moss hung like a lacy curtain from tree branches that reached like fingers across the stream.

Rosetta caught her breath. For a garden fairy, this was a water paradise. She'd flown beside Havendish Stream more times than she could count, but she'd never seen it from a frog's-eye view before. "It's beautiful!" she yelled over to Fawn.

Fawn pulled Swiftlegs's reins to the left, and she and the frog splashed through the shallow water. A school of silver minnows swam away, flashing beneath the surface.

Rosetta yanked on Strongjump's reins. She must not have done it the right way, because the bullfrog stopped short, bucking violently. Rosetta's right foot slipped off his shoulder, and she tumbled into the air.

"Rosetta, what are you doing?" Fawn called, pulling Swiftlegs to a stop.

"Falling!" Rosetta cried. A pretty little violet-petal shoe flew off. It arced toward the edge of the stream. "My shoe!" she shrieked. Beating her wings, Rosetta righted herself and dove after the shoe.

Don't let it hit the water, she thought. The shoe was so close to the stream that she could see its reflection in the surface. She reached out—

Splash!

"Hey," Fawn said from the back of her bullfrog. "Good job—you got it."

Rosetta's hand was raised over her head. In it she held a perfectly dry rabbit-fur-lined shoe. Unfortunately, though, the rest of her—including her *other*

shoe—had landed in Havendish Stream. Her wings felt heavy on her back. They had soaked up water. Now they were too wet for her to fly.

"Yes," Rosetta said. She wiped her sopping hair out of her eyes. "I got the shoe."

Fawn hopped off Swiftlegs's back. She helped Rosetta stand up. Mud squished ickily through the toes of Rosetta's bare foot. "Are you okay?" Fawn asked.

Rosetta took a deep breath. *This isn't Fawn's fault,* she thought. *I said I would do whatever she wanted for a whole day.* "I'm fine," she said.

"I don't think we should do any more frog-riding. Not until you dry out." Fawn eyed Rosetta's soggy wings.

"Oh, that's too bad." Rosetta tried to sound disappointed. Secretly, she was happy not to have to go frog-riding anymore. She couldn't wait to get back to her room. All she wanted was to change into some dry clothes and fix her ruined hair. "Should we go back to the Home Tree?"

Fawn's eyebrows shot up. "Of course not!" she cried. "Our fun day isn't over!"

Rosetta gulped. *Oh, no. We have to have more fun?* she thought.

"Maybe we should go strawberry picking," Fawn suggested. "That's something we can do without flying."

Strawberries? That didn't sound so bad. In fact, Rosetta loved sweets. "We could bring them to the baking-talent fairies," she said. "And maybe we'll have berry pie for dessert tonight."

"Great idea." Fawn grinned.

"Should we go to my garden?" Rosetta suggested. "I've got lots of strawberries."

"Wild berries taste better," Fawn said.

"I don't know about that," Rosetta huffed. But she didn't want to argue about it. After all, this was supposed to be Fawn's special day.

"*Ribbit?*" Swiftlegs said. Next to him, Strongjump was sunning himself on a lily pad.

"We've finished," Fawn told them in frog language. "See you soon!"

"WHERE DID YOU say you saw those strawberries, again?" Rosetta asked. She picked her way around a mud puddle.

"At the edge of the woods, near the golden pine." Fawn fluttered ahead and then darted back. "Not much farther!"

Fawn fluttered off again. She kept doing that. She'd fly ahead to point out an interesting mushroom, or a rock that looked like a funny face, or a beehive— and leave Rosetta behind.

Rosetta kept her eyes glued to Fawn. She didn't want to lose sight of her friend. After all, the farther into the forest they went, the darker it got. Fawn was used to having adventures in the woods, but Rosetta wasn't. It wouldn't be fun to get lost!

Rip!

"Oh, hazelnuts!" Rosetta cried. A piece of her red skirt was caught on the tiny, fierce thorns of a prickleberry bush. Carefully, Rosetta pulled the piece of petal from the bush. One of the thorns pricked her finger. "Ouch!" she cried. Rosetta held up the petal scrap.

She wasn't sure whether the sewing-talent fairies could fix her skirt, but it was worth asking them. She put the piece into her pocket.

"I see them!" Fawn shouted. "There they are!"

Looking up, Rosetta realized that she could no longer see her friend. "Fawn!" she cried. "Where are you?"

"Over here!" Fawn called.

"Over where?" Rosetta asked.

"Follow my voice!"

Rosetta let out a sigh. She shook her wings, but they still weren't completely dry. She hardly ever had to walk anywhere. She wasn't used to it. As she took another step, her dainty shoe stuck in the mud, and her toes slipped right out of it. "Oh, no—my one good shoe!" she said. She hopped backward to try to pick up the shoe, but her heavy wings threw her off balance.

Rosetta flailed her arms.

Plop!

She fell face-first into the mud puddle.

"Rosetta!" Fawn cried, flying into view just overhead. "Are you all right?"

Rosetta gritted her teeth. "I'm fine." She grabbed her shoe. It was, of course, covered in mud. Just like the front of her dress.

She slipped her muddy shoe onto her foot. It squished as she walked. *At least it matches the one that got wet in the river,* she thought.

"Oh." Fawn nodded. "Well, okay. The berries are right over here! Isn't this great?" With a whoop, Fawn fluttered ahead.

Rosetta took a deep breath. *I'm dirty,* she thought, *my wings are wet, and my skirt is torn. And Fawn doesn't even seem to care. Of course she doesn't. Why should she? She's dry. Her clothes aren't torn. She doesn't have a speck of mud on her.*

A spark of anger flared in Rosetta's heart. She trudged after her friend. Fawn probably wouldn't care if she *were* dirty and wet and wearing a torn dress. She'd *still* think this dumb adventure was fun.

Rosetta imagined herself in a fairy bath full of sweet-smelling bubbles. Of course, her wings would stay dry, propped out of the tub as she soaked in the warm water. *Ahh. . . .*

"Right here!" Fawn called. She was hovering beside a golden tree. A large spiderweb was strung between the branch and the trunk. When Rosetta caught up, Fawn pointed to a green leaf the size of a fairy umbrella. Below it was a plump, red wild strawberry speckled with seeds. The sun shone on the berry patch, making the ripe fruit glisten.

"And look!" Fawn added. "We can each carry one back to Dulcie! She can probably make ten pies with these."

Rosetta's mouth watered at the thought. Maybe the day wouldn't turn out to be so horrible after all.

"I have an idea," Fawn said suddenly. "Let's split one!" She picked a strawberry and held it out to Rosetta. "You first."

Rosetta smiled and took a bite. The fruit was sweet and warm from the sun. Rosetta felt better after a single mouthful. She handed the strawberry back to Fawn and sat down on a toadstool.

"It's nice to be in the sunshine," Rosetta said. She tested her wings. They were finally dry.

"It sure is," Fawn agreed. She sat down next to Rosetta. "See? Isn't this a terrific day?" she asked.

Rosetta was about to say yes. But at that moment, a spider dropped right in front of her face.

Rosetta flew two feet in the air, screeching. "Eek! Get it away! Get it away from me!"

Fawn started laughing so hard that she fell off her toadstool.

"Help!" Rosetta shrieked.

"It's just a baby spider," called Fawn.

"That's easy for you to say!" Rosetta shouted back. "It didn't attack you!"

Fawn flew over to her friend and put a hand on her shoulder. "Rosetta, it's okay," she said.

Whimpering, Rosetta hovered as Fawn caught the small green spider. She placed it on the trunk of the golden tree. "Go on," Fawn told the spider. "Go back to your web."

The little spider skittered up the tree. But when Fawn turned to face her friend, she saw that Rosetta wasn't smiling. Not at all. In fact, she looked furious.

"What's wrong?" Fawn asked.

"I can't believe you care more about that spider than you do about me!" Rosetta cried.

Fawn's eyes widened. "What?"

"This has been the worst day ever!" Rosetta griped. "I got all wet. I fell in the mud. I ruined my dress. Then a creepy, crawly spider attacked me—and you just laughed!"

"But—but—we're having fun," Fawn sputtered.

"No, we aren't!" Rosetta cried. "Maybe you're having fun, but I'm having a horrible time! I want to go home!"

Fawn looked surprised. For a moment, she didn't speak.

Tears sparkled in Rosetta's eyes.

"Okay, Rosetta," Fawn said at last. "Let's go home."

9

"Oh, look, Rosetta!" Fawn dove toward a tree with red leaves. A vine with small silver flowers climbed up the trunk. "Angel blooms!"

Rosetta usually loved seeing beautiful flowers. And angel blooms were very rare—even in Pixie Hollow. But Rosetta barely glanced at the flowers. "That's nice," she said. She flew on toward the Home Tree.

Fawn bit her lip. "One of these would look really pretty in your hair," she said.

Rosetta just shrugged and kept flying.

Fawn fluttered after her. "Hey," she said suddenly, "do you want to collect some honey? I know a hive that isn't too far from here."

Rosetta shuddered at the thought of sticky honey. She knew Fawn was trying to cheer her up. But the only things that would improve her mood were a bath, a change of clothes, and a new pair of shoes. "I'd rather just go home."

Fawn nodded slowly. "Okay."

The two flew side by side in silence for a while. They were almost at the edge of the forest when they heard a low coo, then another. The sound seemed to be coming from a nearby tree.

"What's that?" Fawn asked.

Rosetta pretended not to hear her.

"*Coo, coo.*" Peeking into a hole in the wood, Fawn saw three huge pairs of eyes. They were surrounded by soft, dark feathers. Three baby owls blinked up at her. One of them hooted, asking a question.

"Oh, how lovely!" Fawn cried. All fairies—even animal-talent fairies—were afraid of grown owls. But these babies were adorable! "Rosetta!" she called. "You have to see this!"

Rosetta rolled her eyes. "What now?" she muttered.

"You three stay right there," Fawn told the babies, who cooed at her. "Rosetta! Rosetta!" she called. Quick as a flash, she darted after her friend. But she was distracted by the owls. She ran into a tree branch.

"Oof!" Fawn dropped to the ground . . . right into a mole hole!

Rosetta turned. But she hadn't seen what had happened to Fawn. As far as she knew, Fawn had just vanished. "Where did that fairy go?" she mumbled. Rosetta looked inside the hole in the tree. "Oh, how sweet," she said when she saw the three fuzzy owls. "This must be what Fawn wanted me to see! Fawn?" she called, but she still didn't see her friend. "Fawn?"

"Down here!" cried Fawn.

Rosetta flew toward the ground. "Where are you?"

"I'm under your feet!" Fawn called.

Looking down, Rosetta noticed a large hole. She peeked inside. Fawn was in there. Her face was streaked with dirt. "Are you all right?" Rosetta asked.

"I'm not hurt," Fawn said. "But I'm stuck! My wings are trapped. Can you help me out?" She stretched out a hand, but she was still more than a fairy arm's length from the edge of the hole.

Rosetta was about to reach for her friend's hand when a big, ugly black beetle scrambled out of the hole. Then she noticed that there were worms— creepy, crawly, slimy worms—oozing out of the dirt over Fawn's head.

Rosetta jumped to her feet and grimaced. "I can't," she said.

"You can't?" Fawn sounded confused. "Why not?"

Rosetta looked at the beetle and the

worms. Oooh, they were so icky! But she didn't want to tell Fawn the truth. Fawn probably thought that worms and beetles weren't gross at all.

She'll just tell me not to be afraid, like she did with the spider, Rosetta thought. *Or she'll laugh again.* "I—I can't reach you," Rosetta said.

"You can if you lean into the hole a little," Fawn said.

Rosetta shook her head.

Fawn looked at her friend for a moment. "Is it because of the worms?" she asked.

Rosetta wanted to say *No, no, of course not.* But she just couldn't lie to Fawn. "Yes!" she wailed, bursting into tears.

"It's okay, Rosetta," Fawn said. "I understand."

Rosetta was so surprised that she stopped crying. "You do?"

"Sure I do," Fawn said. "We're friends, aren't we? Don't worry, Rosetta. I'm not afraid of worms. I'll be fine here in the hole for a while. Why don't you just go get one of the other animal-talent fairies? Beck could help me out of here."

Rosetta heaved a huge sigh of relief. "Great idea!" she said. "I'll fly like the wind!"

"I'll be waiting," Fawn said.

Rosetta scrambled to her feet and shot into the air—then she stopped. She looked down at the mole hole. She could see Fawn's small face looking up at her.

Wait a minute, Rosetta thought. *What am I doing? Fawn is my friend! I can't just leave her alone in a dark, wormy hole.*

Can I?

Rosetta dropped back to the ground and kneeled at the edge. "Shoo!" she said, waving at the beetle. Once it had waddled off, she stuck her face near the hole. "Okay, Fawn. I'm going to help you out!"

"You don't have to do this," Fawn called. "You can just fly for help, like you did with the squirrel."

"That was different," Rosetta told her. "I'm not an animal talent. I couldn't even talk to him! Besides, you're not a squirrel. You're my friend."

Taking a deep breath, Rosetta stuck her hand into the hole. She whimpered as her fingers touched a slimy worm. It wriggled under her hand, and Rosetta's whimper turned into a moan.

Don't think about it, she told herself.

Slowly, she forced her hand deeper into the hole. *Don't think about how gross it is!* Now she could feel worms all along the length of her arm.

Ooh, but it's so *gross*, she thought.

"Almost there!" Fawn called.

Rosetta closed her hand on something that felt like Fawn's hand—until it squirmed. Rosetta's neck went cold. She wanted to run away. Instead, she forced herself to reach farther.

"Got it!" Fawn cried.

Rosetta felt Fawn's strong hand in hers.

"Now pull!" Fawn called.

Rosetta strained her wings and used both arms to try to drag Fawn out of the hole. Nothing happened.

Rosetta pulled harder. She flapped with all her might. Finally, Fawn broke free. She popped out of the hole so suddenly that both fairies tumbled backward. They landed in a bed of soft moss.

Fawn propped herself up on her arms and looked at her friend. "Are you okay?"

Rosetta blinked twice. "I think so," she said. Then she started to giggle. "I saved you from the worms!"

Fawn laughed, too. "You did! I can't believe it, but you did."

Rosetta sat up and put her arm around Fawn's shoulders. "That's what friends are for," she said.

10

"Ahh," Rosetta said. She stepped into a fresh rose-petal dress. "That's better." She raked a comb through her damp hair and smiled at herself in the mirror.

When she had first stepped into the bath, Rosetta had been sure that she'd never be able to wash away the feel of the slimy worms. But the moment she scrubbed the last bit of dirt from between her toes, she felt like a whole new fairy.

Outside her window, the sky glowed purple behind red and gold clouds. The sun was about to dip below the horizon.

As she slipped her foot into a dainty mole-fur slipper, a birch-bark butterfly flew up to her window. She held out her hand. The butterfly landed, unfolding into a card.

Rosetta read the invitation. "Queen Clarion wants to see me right away?" she cried. "But I don't even have time to put on a fancy gown!" She groaned and cast a glance at the sunset outside her window. *Just when this horrible day was almost over,* she thought.

Rosetta grimaced and fluttered out

of her room. She didn't want to see anyone—not even the queen.

When Rosetta got to the queen's quarters, Fawn was already there. It looked like she was trying not to grin.

"Ah, Rosetta," Queen Clarion said, "come have a cup of tea with us."

Rosetta felt a stab of envy. Fawn was having tea with the queen? Still, Rosetta made her way over to the table. It was set with white linens of the finest spider silk. Plates were heaped with poppy puff rolls, tiny cucumber-seed sandwiches, and sweet honey cakes.

"Have one of these," Fawn said. She held out a plate of small strawberry tarts. "They're made with the wild strawberry we picked today!"

"They are?" Rosetta bit into the crumbly tart. It was even more delicious than she had imagined it would be.

"Fawn has been telling me the most exciting story," Queen Clarion said. She paused to take a sip of rose-hip tea.

"Really?" Rosetta tried to sound interested. She hoped she wouldn't have to sit and listen to another story about Fawn riding a turtle or a groundhog or a bat. *Why would Queen Clarion invite me here for that?* she wondered.

"She tells me that you rescued her," the queen said. Her lips curved into a smile.

"What?" Rosetta's teacup clattered against her saucer. "No, no—she fell into a hole and I helped her out, that's all."

"She made it sound much more dangerous than that," the queen said.

"It was a very deep hole," Fawn said quickly. "And it was full of worms."

"That must have been very frightening," Queen Clarion said to Rosetta.

"Well, it was," Rosetta admitted. "But most fairies wouldn't have been afraid of a few worms."

"The question is not what other fairies would be afraid of," the queen said reasonably. "The question is what *you* were afraid of, and how brave you managed to be for your friend."

Rosetta was quiet. She looked down at her hands. How could she have been brave when she had been terribly scared the whole time?

"Therefore, because you were so brave, I would like to give you this." Queen Clarion reached into a blue silk bag and pulled out a silver necklace. It was just like the one Fawn wore around her neck.

"It's beautiful," Rosetta said as the queen held it up.

"You've earned it, Rosetta," the queen said. She placed her teacup on the table and fluttered over to help Rosetta with the clasp. "There's something else I'd like to show you." Queen Clarion beckoned Rosetta to the window.

Rosetta gasped at what she saw. Fairies—hundreds of them—were gathered below. When they saw Rosetta, they cheered.

"We didn't have time to prepare dinner in Buttercup Canyon," the queen explained. "But I've asked the cooking-talent fairies to serve dinner in the courtyard. And you'll be the guest of honor, Rosetta."

Rosetta looked at Fawn, who smiled a little sheepishly. "I wanted to make sure that your special dinner happened today, before sundown," Fawn said. "I know our adventure wasn't very much fun for you. I thought dinner would make up for it."

"Why?" Rosetta asked.

"Well, I wanted you to have as much fun today as I had yesterday," Fawn said.

"But I didn't do anything as brave as what you did," Rosetta told her friend.

"That isn't true. What you did was very brave," Fawn said. "Everyone has different fears."

"You're not afraid of anything," Rosetta pointed out.

"Sure I am! I'm afraid of dandelion dresses and perfume and fancy dinners," Fawn said. She squeezed Rosetta's hand. "I'm afraid of tearing spider-silk stockings and of having my braid fall into the soup. That dinner was terrifying!"

Rosetta thought about that. For Fawn, putting out the fire had been easy . . . as easy as slipping into a new dress was for Rosetta. It was strange to think that they could be so different and still be such good friends.

"Don't worry, Fawn," Rosetta said.

"I'll always help you with dresses and dinners and things like that."

"And worms?" Fawn asked.

Rosetta shuddered. "Maybe you should ask Beck to handle the worms from now on."

"Shall we go to dinner?" Queen Clarion suggested.

Rosetta and Fawn followed Queen Clarion to the courtyard. How things had changed in a few hours! It had been a truly horrible day. Rosetta thought about her ruined shoes, her muddy dress, the scary spider, and the creepy worms. But there had been some lovely parts, too. She'd never forget how pretty Havendish Stream looked from the back of a frog. Or how wonderful a wild strawberry tasted when you picked it yourself.

She fingered the silver necklace around her neck. Could the worst day of a fairy's life also be the best? *I never knew that a horrible day could become so nice,* she thought. *But it just did.*